For Ari

A TEMPLAR BOOK

First published in the UK in 2021 by Templar Books,
an imprint of Bonnier Books UK,
The Plaza, 535 King's Road, London, SW10 0SZ
Owned by Bonnier Books,
Sveavägen 56, Stockholm, Sweden
www.templarco.co.uk
www.bonnierbooks.co.uk

1 3 5 7 9 10 8 6 4 2

ISBN 978-1-78741-916-2 (Hardback)
ISBN 978-1-78741-987-2 (Paperback)

Designed by Genevieve Webster
Edited by Alison Ritchie
Production by Emma Kidd

Printed in China

This book belongs to:

Sam Usher

LOST

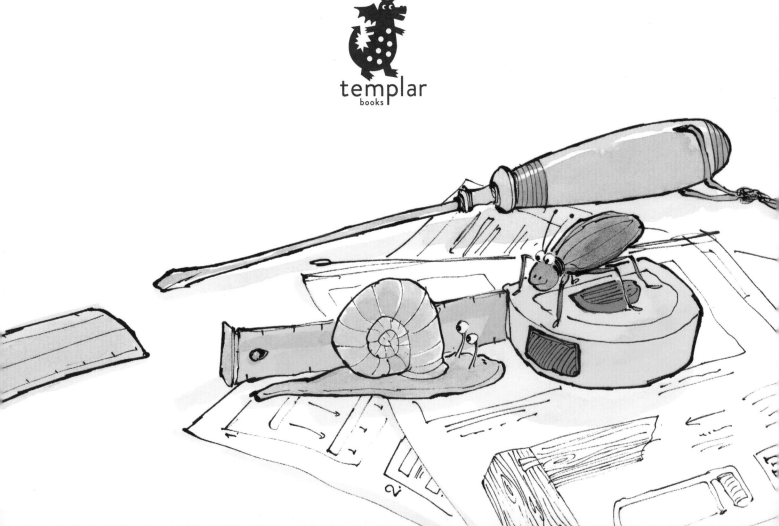

This morning
when I woke up,
it was all grey
and cold and
miserable.

I said, "Grandad, I want to do absolutely
nothing all day."

Grandad said,
"We've just got a few errands to run . . .

and you never know, we might have some fun!"

First we went to the glasses shop.

I said, "Why do you need spectacles, Grandad?"

And he said, "Because I have some very important
reading to do."

Next we went to the library.

I said, "What do you need from here, Grandad?"
And he said, "We have some very important instructions to find."

Then we went to the tool shop.

I said, "What are we doing here, Grandad?"
And he said, "We have something very
important to make."

So we took home
our important equipment.

We were ready to begin!

We plotted.

And measured.

And bent.

And twizzled and tapped.

It took absolutely ages . . .

But it was worth it!

I said, "Grandad, it's the best sledge ever!"

"And look at all that snow, Grandad!
Can we try it out now?"

So we set off.

And on the way we saw something.
I said, "Look, Grandad, there's a note!"

It said **LOST**: LOOPY
PLEASE HELP FIND HER.
REWARD: **CAKE**

We tried calling out for Loopy.
But there was no sign of her . . .

. . . so we carried on walking.

The wind picked up.

Snow was falling everywhere.

So we found shelter.

We carried on calling just in case.
And we stayed until the blizzard stopped
and the sky cleared.

Then we heard something . . .

And Grandad said, "What was THAT?!"

It was Loopy with her new friends!

And they took us
all the way home.

When we got back,
Grandad said,
"If you're lost,
you never know
who you might
turn to for help."
And I agreed.

I hope we go out
again tomorrow.